MW00815363

Grummit's Day

Story by

Paul Cline

Paintings by

Patricia Graham Rogers &

Paul Cline

A Peter Smith Book for

MEDLICOTT PRESS

To Grummit, Emma, Big Red, Dudley &

all the cats who have allowed us to share their lives.

For Dad, who sent me to school. P. G. R.

1 3 5 7 9 10 8 6 4 2
Hardbound ISBN 9625261-3-4
Library of Congress Catalog Card Number 90-063349

A Medlicott Press Book
Distributed by Green Tiger Press
Simon & Schuster Building
1230, Avenue of the Americas
New York, New York 10020

First Edition

Manufactured in
Hong Kong

"Today I feel sad.
I think I've lost something.
I can't remember what it was,
but I know it is important."

"No, it's not in here,

or out here."

"I'm not asking him because he eats everything he finds."

"Somehow I don't think *he* knows where anything is."

"Oh, oh! There's the terrible twins and Spot just waiting to cause trouble. I'd better go back and look indoors again."

“My friend Winslow wouldn’t know.
He’s too busy playing around.”

"Ah well, time for my nap."

"I'll have a good stretch and start looking again."

"No, I didn't lose it in there."

"I would ask him but he always pulls my tail."

"Oh dear, what shall I do?"

"Hello, here's Hilary.
Today was her first day at nursery school."

"Have you been good Grummit?"
"Oh yes Hilary."

"I really missed you Grummit."

"I really missed you Hilary."

"Ah, my dinner. Thank you Hilary."

"This tastes *so* good."

"I always like being clean and dry.
Especially dry."

"Thank goodness I don't have to keep changing *my* fur."

"Oh Grummit, I do love you."

"I love you too Hilary."

"So this is what I've been looking for all day. Love. Love and cuddles. It is silly to think you can lose love because you can never lose it. It's always around somewhere, just waiting for us. Well I've had a busy day. Goodnight and sweet dreams to you all."